Happy

Sad

Titles in the Bunch:

First published in Great Britain 1999 by Mammoth
an imprint of Egmont Children's Books Limited
239 Kensington High Street, London W8 6SA
Published in hardback by Heinemann Library,
a division of Reed Educational and Professional Publishing Limited
by arrangement with Egmont Children's Books Limited.
Text copyright © Pippa Goodhart 1999
Illustrations © Stephen Lambert 1999
The Author and Illustrator have asserted their moral rights.
Paperback ISBN 0 7497 3336 5
Hardback ISBN 0 434 80278 6
10 9 8 7 6 5 4 3
A CIP catalogue record for this title is available from the British Library.
Printed at Oriental Press Limited, Dubai.

Pippa Goodhart

Happy Sad

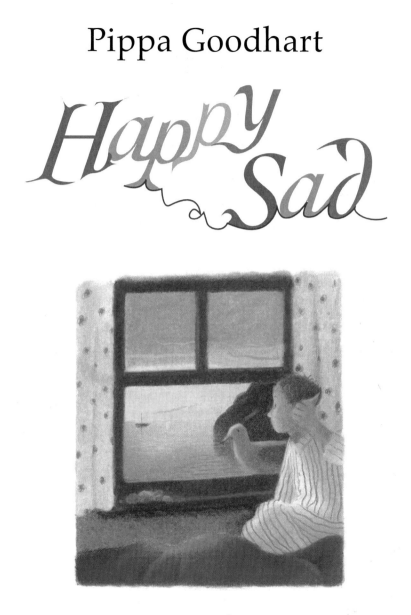

Illustrated by Stephen Lambert

Blue Bananas

For

my friend Pauline

P.G.

To

Sarah, with love

S.L.

Toby lived by the sea. He loved it.
From his bedroom window he could
watch people on the sand and boats
on the water.

I can see the sea.

On stormy days Toby walked in the wind
and watched the waves crashing
on the rocks.

On sunny days Toby took his sisters,

Daisy and Ellen, to the beach.

He chased them with wet seaweed.

When they were tired they made

sandcastles and ate sandy sandwiches.

But sometimes Toby liked to be alone with the sea. He liked to be there when the tide went out, leaving seaweed and surprises from its underwater world.

Wow!

Toby kept things he found from the sea.

He had a starfish

and a crab claw

and lots of shells.

Look what I've found.

He even had a coconut.

One day Toby found a fishy tail flipping in a rock pool. He dipped in his net and fished out a mermaid.

10

Tears dripped down the mermaid's face.

'Why are you sad?' asked Toby.

'Because the tide pulled the sea away

and left me here!' cried the mermaid.

I want to go home.

'Never mind,' said Toby.

'You come home

with me.'

13

So Toby gently lifted the mermaid and put her in his bag. Then he carried her home to show his family.

'What a pretty little thing,' said Mum,

giving the mermaid a cuddle.

'Let's get some water for her, to make her

feel at home,' said Dad.

So Dad filled the paddling

pool with water and

put the mermaid in.

She flipped her tail and swam

round the pool.

Look, a
fountain.

Toby's sisters splashed and played with her.

Toby asked the mermaid, 'Are you happy now?'

'Oh, I am happy sad,' said the mermaid. 'I like the pool, but I miss my friends the fishes. In the sea, they used to swim and sing with me.'

'I'll get you a fish,' said Toby, and he took his money and went to the stalls on the seafront. He threw hoops and won a fish to be a friend for his mermaid.

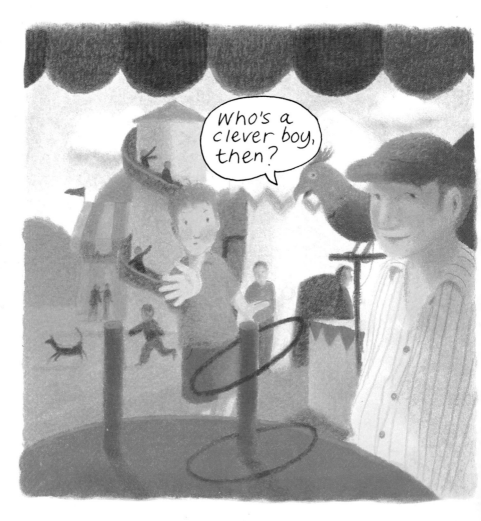

Toby hurried home with

the little orange fish in a bag.

Toby tipped the fish

plop

into the pool.

I've brought
you a friend.

Then he sat on the grass with his sisters
to watch. The little orange fish flipped its
tail and swam round the pool.

22

The mermaid sang a wavy
wild song and splashed
the fish. But the
little fish just swam
round and round.
It didn't sing and
it didn't play.

Oh, the song of the silvery sea.

'Are you happy now?' asked Toby.

'I'm happy sad,' said the mermaid. 'I like the fish, but I miss, oh I miss, my father the sea. The salty, wavy sea that used to toss and play with me.'

'I'll make the pool like the sea,' said Toby, and he ran into the bathroom to get some seaweed shampoo.

He went to his bedroom to pick up some

shells and stones.

Then he went down to the kitchen

for a pot of salt.

Toby ran back to the pool. He tipped in
the shells and stones, the salt and seaweed
shampoo. Then he put his hands into the
water and stirred up waves and wildness.

What's he doing now?

'Are you happy now?' asked Toby.

'I'm still happy sad,' said the mermaid. 'I like the wildness, but I miss, oh I miss, my mother the sea. She used to rock me and sing me to sleep.'

'I can do that,' said Toby. He picked up

the mermaid. He held her in his arms.

He rocked her and he sang sleepy songs.

I miss my family.

But a tear ran down the mermaid's cheek.

'Oh, dear,' said Toby. 'Only the sea can make you happy. I'll take you home.'

Toby's family waved goodbye as Toby

carried the little mermaid over

the sand to the sea.

Take care,
little mermaid.

'Goodbye,' said Toby. 'I hope you will be happy now.'

The mermaid smiled. 'I am happy sad,' she said. 'I am happy because the salty wavy sea is my home. But I am sad to say goodbye to you. Why don't you come and live in the sea with me, Toby?

Then I won't be sad at all.'

Come and meet my family.

Toby thought of having fishes for friends.

He thought of meeting Father sea and

Mother sea.

It would be fun living

with his mermaid friend.

But then Toby thought of his own father and mother.

He thought of leaving his little sisters.

He thought of his home

and his room, and he

shook his head.

'I want to go back to

my home too,' he said.

So the mermaid flipped her tail and

swam into the sea.

She dived down,

down,

down

and away.

Toby was sad as he watched her go,

but he was happy too. He was pleased

that the mermaid was happy.

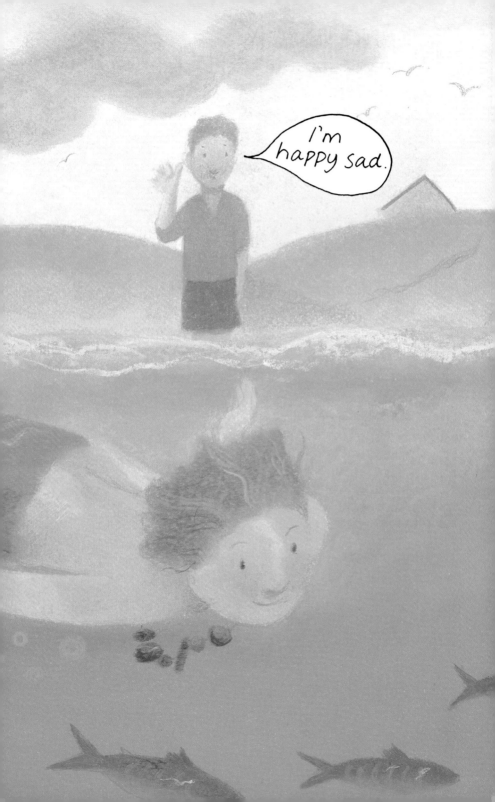

Toby went back home. Daisy and Ellen were waiting for him. 'Let's play mermaid and fishes,' they said.

Then it was bedtime and Dad chased them indoors. When Toby was tucked up in bed, Mum sang him a mermaid song.

When Mum had said goodnight and gone downstairs, Toby listened to his big seashell and thought about the mermaid.

He looked out of his window at the
empty sand and sea. He looked along
the golden path of moonlight and saw
something. Was it the flick of a tail?
Could it be the wave of a hand?

I'm like the mermaid, thought Toby. I am happy sad. But the mermaid will always be my friend. Perhaps she will come back and play with me again.

And he snuggled down
in bed and went to sleep.